For Donna, Emily, Suzy,
Christopher, and Charlotte KW

For the National Federation
of Badger Groups CW

OXFORD
UNIVERSITY PRESS

Great Clarendon Street, Oxford OX2 6DP

Oxford University Press is a department of the University of Oxford.
It furthers the University's objective of excellence in research, scholarship,
and education by publishing worldwide in

Oxford New York

Athens Auckland Bangkok Bogotá Buenos Aires Calcutta
Cape Town Chennai Dar es Salaam Delhi Florence Hong Kong Istanbul
Karachi Kuala Lumpur Madrid Melbourne Mexico City Mumbai
Nairobi Paris São Paulo Singapore Taipei Tokyo Toronto Warsaw

with associated companies in Berlin Ibadan

Oxford is a registered trade mark of Oxford University Press
in the UK and in certain other countries

British Library Cataloguing in Publication Data available

ISBN 0–19–279024–2 (hardback)
ISBN 0-19-272346-4 (paperback)

Typeset by Darren Hayward
Printed in Hong Kong

If you would like to help badgers in Britain, please write to:
The National Federation of Badger Groups
15 Cloisters Business Park
8 Battersea Park Road, London SW8 4BG

KATHRYN WHITE

Good Day, Bad Day

Illustrated by Cliff Wright

OXFORD
UNIVERSITY PRESS

W hen they fight,

the world shakes.

The house quakes.

Beasts roar

and beat on the door.

It gets dark and I am lost.

It gets cold
and I shiver.

Mighty monsters
make me quiver.

I am a ship in
stormy seas.

I am a kite, blown
away in a breeze.

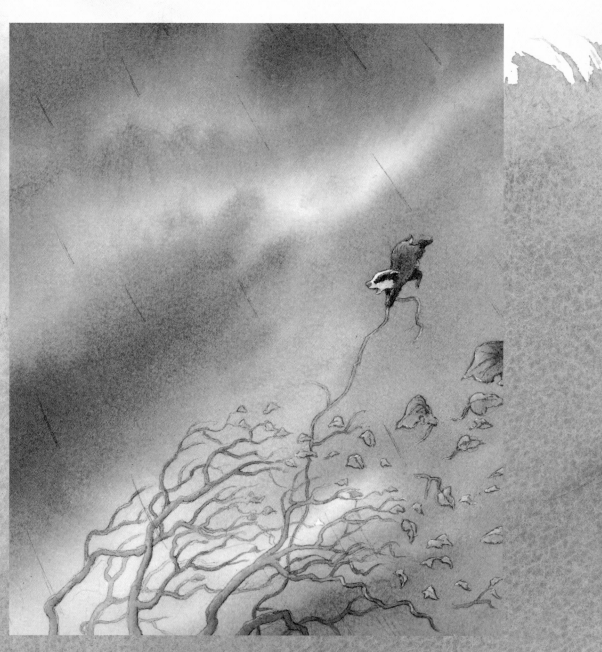

Will I ever see
home again?

When they are friends
the sun comes out.

I float on the clouds.

I am as strong as a lion.

I can run as fast as a tiger.

I can jump as high as the moon.

I can sing. I can dance.

I shout, I can do anything.

The world smiles.

I am safe.
I am warm in a cosy nest.

I am happy. I am precious.

I love my Mum and Dad,
and I know they love me.